THE NUTCRACKER

Re-told by Anne McKie. Illustrated by Ken McKie.

This enchanting tale took place
almost a century ago. It is a story full
of fantasy and perhaps a little magic.
You may think it was all just a dream
or did it really happen?

Every Christmas Eve, Mayor Stahlbaum
gave a grand party for his son and
daughter and all their young friends.

Now Mayor Stahlbaum was a very rich man, and young Fritz and Clara had a huge nursery full of expensive and unusual toys.

Clara had so many different dolls - she couldn't remember all their names. While her brother Fritz had too many soldiers to count! These soldiers were kept in a model fort twice as high as Fritz himself!

At last it was Christmas Eve and the party was in full swing. Clara and Fritz and their young guests eagerly unwrapped the presents that lay beneath the sparkling Christmas tree.

What fun it was. The children joined in all the games and dancing. They made so much noise the grown-ups felt quite tired out.

It was on that night that a very strange guest arrived at the party. It was Herr Drosselmeyer, Clara's godfather. He was a rather odd old gentleman who made fantastic toys, so life-like, the children were almost afraid to touch them.

Clara and Fritz were never quite sure if they were real or not.

This Christmas Eve, the old man had brought a very special present for Clara. It was a Nutcracker doll in the shape of a soldier.

"This is my favorite Christmas present of all!" cried Clara with delight. "Isn't my Nutcracker handsome?" and she held up her doll for all to see.

"I think he's the ugliest thing I ever saw!" shouted
Clara's brother. It was getting late and young Fritz was
tired (and had eaten far too many sweets.)

"Give it to me!" he whined. Quick
as a flash Fritz grabbed the Nutcracker,
pushed a huge hazelnut into its mouth
and jammed it shut.

There was a loud crack and the doll's head was split.
The nut rolled out and Fritz flung the Nutcracker onto the
floor in temper.

Near to tears, Clara picked up her broken Nutcracker.
But Herr Drosselmeyer gently tied his handkerchief round
the doll's head and whispered, "In the morning it will be
handsome once more!"

Late that night, when all the house was asleep, Clara crept down to the nursery.

As the clock struck midnight, Clara glanced up and was very startled to see Herr Drosselmeyer sitting right on the very top.

What a fright Clara got. Far across the floor, from every corner of her nursery, swarms of mice came scampering towards her!

Clara sprang backwards, for the mice looked as big as herself - and so did the soldiers.

As the little girl let out a scream of fright, the soldiers came to life. They blew their bugles and banged their drums and were soon fighting a fierce battle against the mice.

Then Clara gasped in amazement as her Nutcracker doll jumped out of his box as if by magic. He grabbed the nearest sword and joined the soldiers in battle.

All of a sudden from the depth of the army of mice, sprang the evil Mouse King. He had a golden crown on his head and was waving a great sharp sword.

It was quite clear that the mice were winning. There were so many of them.

As the Mouse King came towards the Nutcracker with his sharp sword, Clara pulled off her shoe and aimed it at his head. The shoe caught the Mouse King off guard and he fell to the ground.

Instantly, all the mice vanished, and standing in the
Nutcracker's place - was a handsome prince!

"Come with me, Clara!" said the Nutcracker Prince,
"and I will take you to a wonderful land!"

Without another word, he whisked Clara off through
the wondrous Kingdom of Snow, where the little
snowflakes danced in and out of the glittering trees.

The Nutcracker Prince led Clara by the hand and soon they came to the marvelous Land of Sweets, and there at the palace to greet them was the Sugar Plum Fairy.

"Clara saved me from the wicked Mouse King!" the Prince smiled as he told the Fairy about their battle with the mice.

"You must be a very brave girl!" the Sugar Plum Fairy told Clara. "Sit here in the place of honor and receive our grateful thanks."

With that she led Clara to a marzipan throne next to the Prince, clapped her hands and cried, "Let the celebrations begin!"

First came dancers from Spain and from Arabia - Clara
was enchanted.

Next came acrobats from China and swirling, stamping Cossacks from Russia - Clara was spellbound.

Last of all came the twirling, whirling Flower Dolls that waltzed with the Sugar Plum Fairy - Clara was lost in a world of fantasy.

Then everyone in the Land of Sweets began to wave goodbye, and Clara felt herself floating on a big soft cloud, just like a dream.

Very gently she drifted far away until the Sugar Plum Fairy and the Nutcracker Prince slowly faded, and the magical Land of Sweets was left far behind.

The next thing Clara knew, she was lying on the nursery floor back in her own house and held tightly in her arms was her Nutcracker doll.

The little girl realized it was morning. Had it all been just a lovely dream?

Clara ran to the nursery window. As she looked out that cold Christmas Day, she could just make out the dark figure of Herr Drosselmeyer disappearing down the street in the softly falling snow...